The Boy Who
Drew Birds

To my mother, Ann Davies
—J.D.

To Sally Regan
—M.S.

www.hmhco.com

Library of Congress Cataloging-in-Publication Data

Davies, Jacqueline, 1962–
The boy who drew birds : a story of John James Audubon / Jacqueline Davies ; illustrated by Melissa Sweet.
p. cm.
Includes bibliographical references (p. 31).
ISBN 0-618-24343-7
1. Audubon, John James, 1785-1851–Juvenile literature. 2. Ornithologists–United States–Biography–Juvenile literature. 3. Animal painters–United States–Biography–Juvenile literature. I. Sweet, Melissa, ill. II. Title.
QL31.A9D38 2003
598'.092–dc22

2004000971

Printed in China

SCP 26 25 24 23 22 21
4500815200
The illustrations are mixed media using Twinrocker handmade papers, collage, and found objects. The text is set in Regula.
The display type is set in Escrita.

The Boy Who Drew Birds

A STORY OF JOHN JAMES AUDUBON

by Jacqueline Davies ~

Illustrated by Melissa Sweet

Nº 25.
Alcedo attri
Near Nantes

HOUGHTON MIFFLIN COMPANY ★ BOSTON

It was true that John James could skate, hunt, and ride better than most boys. True also that he could dance the minuet and gavotte as if he had been born a king. He could fiddle, he could flirt, he could fence. But what he liked to do best, from sunup to sundown, was watch birds.

John James's happiest memories were of woodland walks with his father near their home in France. On these walks, Papa Audubon would talk of birds. Their beautiful colors, their graceful flight, and—most wonderful of all—their mysterious disappearance each fall, followed by their faithful return in the spring.

Pres
Nantes

JJA

Wood Thrush 2
Sparrow   2
Redstart   3
Chat   1
Owl   1

But now John James was eighteen years old and he walked through the Pennsylvania woods alone, his father four thousand miles away. Only six months before, his father had put him on a ship. The ship carried John James to America, where he was to live in a farmhouse on the banks of a creek. His father had sent him there to learn English, to learn commerce, to learn how to make money in America. But mostly he had sent away his only son so that John James would not have to fight in Napoleon's war. John James wondered if he would ever see his father again.

It was April in Pennsylvania, and slashes of snow still lay in deep hollows. John James splashed across the icy creek. He scrambled up the bank and approached the limestone cave, wondering what he would find today. Just the empty nest of a pewee bird, as he had found the last five days? Or would there be—

Ffb, Ffb, Ffb! A flurry of wings greeted John James. The pewee flycatchers had returned!

The female bird flew out of the cave like an arrow shot from a bow. The male bird, larger and darker, beat his wings above John James's head and snapped his beak. *Clack, clack, clack!*

John James ran out of the cave and crouched next to the creek. He watched as the birds dipped and soared, snapping up mayflies in flight. *Are these the same pewees who built the nest last year?* he wondered. *Where did they spend the winter? Will they return next spring?*

John James ran home through the woods. *"Madame Thomas! Madame Thomas!"* he shouted, bursting into the farmhouse kitchen. *"Il y a des oiseaux!"* In his excitement, his words tumbled out in French.

Mrs. Thomas was the housekeeper Papa Audubon had hired to take care of Mill Grove, his American farmhouse. She pointed her long wooden spoon at John James's muddy shoes. He quickly took them off and placed them by the fire to dry.

"Birds," he said. "I see birds. Two. In cave. Beautiful!"

Mrs. Thomas frowned. She was fond of this energetic French boy. And yet she had to admit that he was something of a cracked pot. Birds! Always birds! From the moment he woke up in the morning to the moment he closed his eyes at night, he thought only of birds. It was strange for a boy his age.

"Master Audubon," she scolded, "thou wouldst do well to do God's work by tending the farm more and chasing after birds less."

Raising and falling with
such beautiful ease of
motion of the wave that
one might suppose they
receive special powers to
that effect from the
Element below.—

25.

JJA

N° 34.

N° 11
(Passerina ciris)
Painted
Bunting

JJA

Hermit Thrush May 5

Pewee-2 May 10

American Robin - May 6

Scarlet Tanager June 1

Common Crow June 3

Red-Winged Blackbird

Junco May 1

Mockingbird

But John James, halfway up the staircase, pretended not to hear. He climbed straight to his attic room—his *musée*, he called it. Every shelf, every tabletop, every spare inch of floor, was covered with nests and eggs and tree branches and pebbles and lichen and feathers and stuffed birds: redwings and grackles, kingfishers and woodpeckers. The walls were covered with pencil and crayon drawings of birds, all signed "JJA." Every year on his birthday, John James took down these drawings — a year's worth of work — and burned them in the fireplace. He hoped some day he would make drawings worth keeping.

John James went to his
bookcase and took down the
natural history books, gifts
from his father. *Where do small
birds go in the winter? Do the same
birds come back to the same nests each spring?*
The scientists who wrote these books did
not agree; each one gave a different answer.

Two thousand years before, the
Greek philosopher Aristotle had
given his answers to these
questions. Aristotle said that
every fall great flocks of
cranes flew south and
returned in the spring. But
he believed that small birds did
not migrate. Small birds, wrote
Aristotle, hibernated under water or in
hollow logs all winter.

There was a
tangle of birds
in my net
just last week.

They lay under water all winter.

I believe they transform themselves from one bird to another.

Many scientists of the day still agreed with Aristotle. Small birds, they said, gathered themselves in a great ball, clinging beak to beak, wing to wing, and foot to foot, and lay under water all winter, frozen-like. Fishermen even told stories of catching such tangles of birds in their nets.

John James had never, *ever* found a tangled ball of birds under water. And he did not believe everything the scientists said. Why, some of them believed that birds transformed from one kind into another each winter! And one scientist claimed that birds traveled to the moon each fall and returned in the spring. He said the trip took sixty days!

TO THE MOON!?

John James had never spent much time inside a classroom, and he had failed every exam he had taken in school. But he considered himself a naturalist. He studied birds in nature to learn their habits and behaviors.

I will bring my books to the cave, John James decided. *And my pencils and paper. I will even bring my flute. I will study my cave birds every day. I will draw them just as they are.* And because he was a boy who loved the out-of-doors more than the in, that is just what he did.

In a week, the birds were used to him. They ignored him as if he were an old stump. They carried bits of moist mud as he drew with his pencils. They brought in tufts of green moss as he read his French fables. They gathered stray goose feathers from the banks of the creek as he played songs on his flute.

Soon the dried brown nest had become a soft green bed. And John James had learned to imitate the throaty call of the birds: *Fee-bee! Fee-bee!*

feebee ve bliebt fee bee ve

Spring slipped into summer. Summer sighed and became fall. John James watched as two broods of nestlings hatched. He watched as the young birds flew for the first time. He began to feel a part of this small family.

When the days grew shorter and the autumn air began to bite, John James knew the birds would leave soon. But would they come back? He had to know! The question was terribly important to the boy so far from his family.

In bed that night, he formed a plan.

The next day, when the mother and
father birds were away from the nest,
John James picked up one of the
baby birds. He had read of medieval kings
who tied bands on the legs of their prize falcons so that
a lost falcon could be returned. Why not band a wild bird to find out
where it goes? It had never been done, but John James could try.

He pulled a string from his pocket and tied it loosely around the
baby bird's leg. The bird pecked it off. The next day, he tied another
string to the bird's leg. Again the bird pecked it off. Finally, John James
walked five miles to the nearest village and bought some thread woven
of fine strands of silver. This thread was soft and strong. He tied a
piece of it loosely to one leg of each baby bird.

A week later, the birds were gone.

more precious
than diamonds

Nest
mud, moss, fine grasses
under bridges
old sheds
cliffs, on horizontal
or verticle supports
Size: 2 1/2 inches
inside depth 1 3/4"

All winter, John James worked in his *musée*, painting the pencil sketches he had made in the cave. He hoped that on his next birthday he would have one or two pictures worth saving from the fire.

The creek was frozen now, and each time John James skated past the empty cave, he thought of the two-thousand-year-old question: *Where do small birds go, and do they return to the same nest in the spring?*

The days grew longer. The ice on the creek cracked and melted.

One morning, John James heard a bird call, *Fee-bee! Fee-bee!*

He ran to the cave. He ducked his head and stepped inside.

The female bird did *not* fly out of the cave like an arrow shot from a bow.

The male bird did *not* beat his wings above John James's head and snap his beak. Instead, they ignored John James as if he were an old stump. Watching the birds fly in and out of the cave, John James knew that his friends had returned.

But where were last year's babies, now grown? Had they returned, too? He began to search the woods and orchard nearby, listening for their call.

Out in the meadow, inside a hay shed, he found two birds building a nest. One wore a silver thread around its leg.

Up the creek, under a bridge, he found two more nesting birds. And one wore a silver thread around its leg.

John James wanted to shout, "Yes! The same birds return to the same nest! And their children nest nearby." But who would have heard him? *I will write to my father*, he decided. *I will tell him what I have learned in America. And when I am older, I will find a way to tell the whole world.*

He ran back to his house to gather his pencils, paper, and flute.

As he ran, he called, *"Fee-bee! Fee-bee!"*

Cher Papa,

J'espère que tu peux lire cette lettre. J'écris par la lumière d'une bougie que est en train de s'éteindre. J'ai eu une si intéressante expérience aujourd'hui, et je veux bien te le raconter, mon ami depuis toujours.

ABOUT JOHN JAMES AUDUBON

*B*anding a bird — that is, tying a marker around a bird's leg to track its movement — was an innovative idea in Audubon's time. In fact, in 1804 John James became the first person in North America to band a bird. His simple experiment helped prove a complex theory: Many birds return to the same nest each year, and their offspring nest nearby. This behavior is called *homing*. The rest of the world learned of Audubon's experiment when he wrote about it in his book *Ornithological Biography*. Later, in the twentieth century, scientists used bird banding to prove that small birds migrate.

Not long after the story in this book ends, John James returned to France and his father's house. Perhaps he, like the birds, felt a pull toward home. But a year later, he sailed back to America, saying goodbye to Papa Audubon, his "friend through life." It was the last time he saw his father.

The young John James grew to be the greatest painter of birds of all time. He was the first to paint life-size images of birds and the first to show birds hunting, preening, fighting, and flying. His revolutionary paintings pleased two audiences: scientists, who were drawn to their accuracy, and ordinary people, who simply enjoyed the beauty of his birds.

Audubon made hundreds of sketches of his cave birds; none survived. He painted this watercolor of the Pewee Flycatcher (now called Eastern Phoebe) in Louisiana around 1825.

(Collection of The New-York Historical Society)

AUTHOR'S SOURCE NOTE

In writing this story, I relied primarily on John James Audubon's own account in *Ornithological Biography* and Shirley Streshinsky's *Audubon: Life and Art in the American Wilderness*. Nearly every detail included in this story is documented in these two books. Audubon did burn many of his early drawings on his birthday. Where he purchased the silver thread is a matter of speculation, but Audubon regularly walked five miles to the nearest village, Norristown, and it is almost certain that Mrs. Thomas, a sober Quaker, would not have had any silver thread in her sewing basket. Whether or not Audubon read the works of Aristotle is open to question. Papa Audubon loved to give books as gifts, and it is likely that one of the natural history books he gave to his son included the ancient Greek's theories on bird migration and hibernation.

BIBLIOGRAPHY

Audubon, John James. *Writings and Drawings*. Edited by Christoph Irmscher. New York: Library of America, 1999. Includes *Ornithological Biography; Myself; My Style of Drawing Birds;* and *Mississippi River Journal.*

Ford, Alice. *John James Audubon*. Norman: University of Oklahoma Press, 1964.

——, ed. *Audubon, By Himself.* Garden City, N.Y.: Natural History Press, 1969.

Foshay, Ella M. *John James Audubon*. New York: Henry N. Abrams, 1997.

Streshinsky, Shirley. *Audubon: Life and Art in the American Wilderness.* New York: Villard Books, 1993.

Welty, Susan F. *Birds with Bracelets*. Englewood Cliffs, N.J.: Prentice-Hall, 1965.

ILLUSTRATOR'S SOURCE NOTE

In Mill Grove, Pennsylvania, the house and land where this story takes place are now part of the Audubon Wildlife Sanctuary. I spent a couple of days there looking at paintings, roaming the woods, and drawing birds. Alan Gehret, an assistant administrator and curator, patiently answered my questions and showed me original documents. Many thanks to Alan for his time and expertise. Later I went to the John James Audubon State Park in Henderson, Kentucky. The museum there had many more artifacts and art from Audubon's life. Thank you to Don Boarman, the curator, for his help in my research. The bird songs were identified in *Field Book of Wildbirds and Their Music* by F. Schuyler Mathews.

The impressions that stayed with me were surprisingly simple. It would be hard not to be in awe of Audubon's art, but it was the cadence of his handwriting and the quality of the handmade papers he used that became the starting point for my paintings and collages. The art was done on Twinrocker handmade papers and antique papers, with Sennelier watercolors and gouache, pen and ink, pencil, and collage.